What-a-Mess
in
Winter

Frank Muir
Illustrated by Joseph Wright

A Picture Corgi 0 552 52177 9
Printing History.
First published in 1982 by Ernest Benn Limited.
Picture Corgi edition published 1982.
Reprinted 1986.
© Frank Muir 1982.
Illustrations © Joseph Wright 1982.
Picture Corgi Books are published by
Transworld Publishers Ltd.,
61-63 Uxbridge Road, Ealing, London W5 5SA.
Printed in Portugal by Printer Portuguesa

PICTURE CORGI

The weather was bitterly cold. An icy wind shrieked round the house, whistling through the keyholes and keeping the cat door flapping as though a hundred invisible kittens were scampering in and out.

The aristocratic and elegant Afghan Hound puppy, Prince
Amir of Kinjan—known to the world as the fat and scruffy
puppy, What-a-Mess—did not like the cold. He spent as much
time as he could snoozing in his basket, wrapped in a tablecloth
which he pulled off the dining-room table, a drip hanging
permanently on the end of his nose.

"Wake up!" his mother shouted. "You must be the World Snoozer Champion! Why can't you be more like your famous grandfather, the champion hunter of all Afghanistan! *He* didn't snooze all day with a drip on the end of his nose. He was out in the snows hunting snow-leopards for the King. And when he wasn't hunting snow-leopards he stood on a mountain top, guarding the Khyber Pass."

Reluctantly, What-a-Mess climbed out of his basket, shook the drip from his nose (another began forming immediately) and went out into the icy cold of the garden to ask the cat-next-door whether she would mind if he hunted her, as his grandfather had hunted snow-leopards.

"Can't," said the cat-next-door. "I've got to keep tidy. An aunt is coming to tea."

"But you're never *not* tidy!" said the puppy, trying to get rid of a sheet of newspaper which had stuck itself to some jam and mud on his back-legs. "Just a *small* snow-leopard hunt?" he pleaded. "To the dustbin and back?"

"You've got a drip on the end of your nose," said the cat, and walked delicately home.

What-a-Mess, feeling colder than ever, decided that if he could
not hunt snow-leopards like his famous grandfather, then
he had better find a mountain top to guard.
Preferably indoors in the warm.

He thought the top of the stairs was probably a bit like the
Khyber Pass so sat and guarded it proudly. After what seemed
like four hours of guarding, (in fact it was three and a half
minutes) the gallant Afghan puppy fell asleep.

The man who lived in the house failed to see the snoozing puppy, tripped over him, fell down the stairs, knocked three pictures off the wall on his way down and sprained his thumb at the bottom.

The strange thing was that he did not seem to mind. He just laughed. And all the rest of the family laughed too. What-a-Mess thought this odd because they usually shouted at him when he had done something wrong.

This new, happy atmosphere spread over the next few days. A curious air of electric excitement filled the house and the family kept bringing in bright things like wrapping-paper, balloons, holly, and the man kept staggering in with parcels of clinking bottles.

"Not tomorrow," said the girl of the house, eyes shining, "or the day after. Or the day after that. But the day after *that* . . . Christmas is coming!" And she hugged him.

"Who is Christmas?" the puppy asked his mother that night. "And what is he coming here for? Does he like dogs? Or will we be shut away like when the big lady in the hat calls?"

"Christmas isn't a 'he'," his mother explained. "It's the very best day of the whole year!" And she went on to explain all about it. "And do you know what?" she ended with. "Children can tell their mothers what presents they would really like and if they have been good, then Father Christmas comes down the chimney and leaves the presents for the children to find when they wake up on Christmas morning."

What-a-Mess had never heard anything so wonderful in the whole of his short, fat life. "And does this happen to puppies as well, or only to children?" he asked, his heart in his mouth in case it did not happen to puppies.

"Only to *well-behaved* puppies," said his mother.

"I'll be well-behaved!" And he rushed out to his Number One (Winter) Thinking Place—in the rabbbit hutch with the old rabbit Starsky—to think what presents to ask Father Christmas for.

After two days of deep thought he decided on
the following:

A bone. Ox-tail, please. And much too hot for me to bite so
that I have to leave it under my nose to cool down, and the
smell will rise . . .

Two pairs of roller-skates so that I will be able to catch the cat-next-door and pulverise her.

A cat-mint plant. (I do not like the smell of it but that cat-next-door loves it and she has not got any.)

A new nose that will not drip in winter.

A million trillion Doggy Chocolate Drops.

A house of my own the size of the one I live in, only all the
rooms are kitchens and all the furniture is sofas.

A new dog basket with liver-flavoured wickerwork.

A small snow-leopard, without claws and slow on its feet, for hunting purposes.

Something very, very nice that I can give my mother. (If you can't think of anything nice enough, Father Christmas, I could give her half my chocolate drops.)

That night in bed it seemed hours before What-a-Mess's
mother at last asked him what he would like Father Christmas
to bring him.

The puppy drew a deep breath.

"Well . . ." he began. "A bone . . ."

His mother waited. "Is that all?" she asked. "What a good
little puppy you are to ask for something so simple. Are you
sure that is all you want?"

The answer was silence. That was all he *did* ask for.

What-a-Mess, overcome with all that thinking and with the
excitement of Christmas, had fallen fast asleep.